# Oi Dog!

Hodder
Children's
Books

Written by
**Kes & Claire Gray**

Illustrated by
**Jim Field**

OI DOG! GET OFF THE FROG

said the frog.

"But I like sitting on frogs," said the dog.

To Elin K.G.

Oi Evan! Oi Olivia! My biggest *Oi Frog!* fans  J.F

HODDER CHILDREN'S BOOKS
First published in Great Britain in 2016 by Hodder and Stoughton

Text copyright © Kes Gray and Claire Gray, 2016
Illustrations copyright © Jim Field, 2016

A CIP catalogue record for this book is available from the British Library.

HB ISBN: 9781 444 91958 5
PB ISBN: 9781 444 91959 2

10 9 8 7 6 5 4 3 2 1

Printed and bound in China

MIX
Paper from responsible sources
FSC
www.fsc.org   FSC® C104740

Hodder Children's Books
An imprint of Hachette Children's Group
Part of Hodder and Stoughton
Carmelite House
50 Victoria Embankment
London EC4Y 0DZ

An Hachette UK Company
www.hachette.co.uk
www.hachettechildrens.co.uk

www.kesgray.com   www.jimfield.co.uk

"Frogs are all **squishy** and **squashy** and when you sit on them they go PLURPPPPPPPPPPP!"

"You know the rules," said the cat.

**"Cats** sit on **mats, frogs** sit on **logs,** and **dogs** sit on **FROGS!"**

"Well, I'm **changing** the rules," said the frog.

"From now on, **dogs** sit on **logs** not **frogs!**"

"What will **bears** sit on?"
asked the dog.

"**Bears** will sit on **stairs**," said the frog.

"What will **slugs** sit on?"
asked the dog.

"**Slugs** will sit on **plugs**,"
said the frog.

"**Slugs** will sit on **plugs**,
**flies** will sit on **pies**,

crickets will sit on **tickets**,

and **moths** will sit on **cloths**."

"What will **leopards** sit on?" asked the dog.

"**Leopards** will sit on **shepherds**," said the frog.

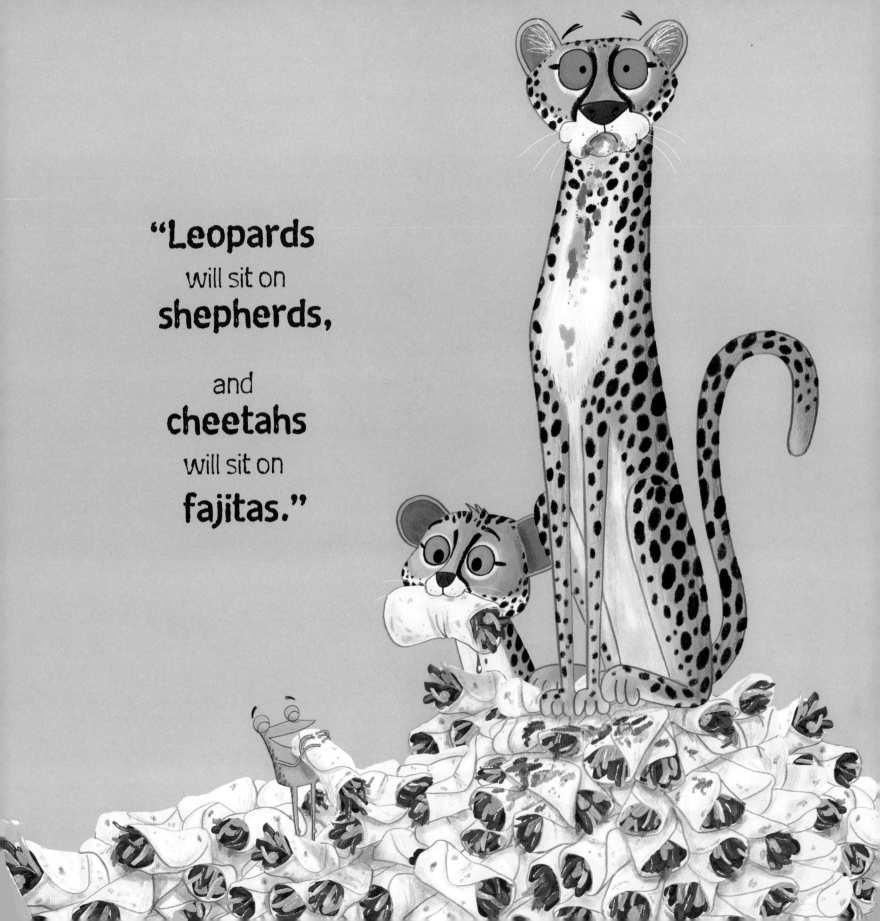

"**Leopards** will sit on **shepherds,**

and **cheetahs** will sit on **fajitas.**"

"You're really getting the hang of this," said the dog.

"I know," said the frog. "And that's not all..."

"What will **whales** sit on?" asked the dog.

**"Whales** will sit on **nails,"** said the frog.

"I'm not sure the whales
will like that," said the dog.

"They don't have to like it," said the frog,
"they just have to do it."

"What will **dragons** sit on?" said the dog.

"**Dragons** will sit on **wagons**," said the frog.

"**Dragons** will sit on **wagons**,

**kittens** will sit on **mittens**,

**mice** will sit on **ice**,

and **puppies** will sit on **guppies**."

"What will **crabs** sit on?" asked the dog.

"**Crabs** will sit on **kebabs,**" said the frog.

"**Crabs** will sit on **kebabs,**

**poodles** will sit on **noodles,**

**hornets** will sit on **cornets,**

**skunks** will
sit on **trunks,**

and
**elephants**
will sit on
**smelly pants!"**

**"Elephants**
aren't going to sit on
**smelly pants!"**
gasped the dog.

"They are now,"
smiled the frog.

"**Hold on,**" said the cat. "If **dogs** sit on **logs,**

**cats** sit on **gnats, bears** sit on **stairs,**

**slugs** sit on **plugs, flies** sit on **pies,**

**crickets** sit on **tickets, moths** sit on **cloths,**

**leopards** sit on **shepherds,**

**cheetahs** sit on **fajitas,**

**gnus** sit on **canoes,**

**pigs** sit on **wigs,**

**boars** sit on **oars,**

**whales** sit on **nails,**

**dragons** sit on **wagons,**

**mice** sit on **ice,**

**kittens** sit on **mittens,**

puppies sit on **guppies,**
**crabs** sit on **kebabs,**
**poodles** sit on **noodles,**
**hornets** sit on **cornets,**
**skunks** sit on **trunks,**
and **elephants** sit on
**smelly pants...**"

WHAT ARE
FROGS
GOING TO
SIT ON?

asked the dog.